9/22

This is for Zachary, with so
much love —R.V.

For Jungmin —H.Y.

ISBN 978-1-338-75116-1 • 10 9 8 7 6 5 4 3 2 1   22 23 24 25 26 • Printed in Mexico 189 • First edition, July 2022 • Hyewon Yum's art was created with colored pencils. The text type was set in Hyewonyum created by Hyewon Yum and Gill Sans • The display type was set in Spicy Rice • The book was printed and bound in Grupo Espinosa. Production was overseen by Catherine Weening • Manufacturing was supervised by Shannon Rice • The book was art directed by Patti Ann Harris, designed by Rae Crawford, and edited by Liza Baker.

a BIG FEELINGS book

Sometimes I Grumblesquinch

by **Rachel Vail** · illustrated by **Hyewon Yum**

Orchard Books
New York
an imprint of Scholastic Inc.

My name is Katie Honors and I'm a really nice kid.
I always go along nicely.

I'm happy to play any game when a friend comes over.
Even if I lose, I am a good sport.
"Good game," I say, either way. I hardly frown.

If there isn't mango sorbet,
I say,
"That's okay, I like cookie dough, too."

Mom smiles and says I can get sprinkles,
which is extra. I didn't even ask.

"Katie is such a pleasure," Mom says.

"She really is," Dad agrees.

I fit perfectly in their hugs.
They are very proud of me.
But there is something they don't know.

Some mornings, my little brother, Chuck, crawls into my bed while I am still sleeping.
He breathes hot on my eyelid.

A drool from his wet mouth plonks onto my arm.

The first word I say in the whole day is "Ew!"
I say it very quietly, though.

I put on my beautiful new shirt.
I love it. It cheers me right up.

Chuck follows me down to breakfast
and sits in my seat.

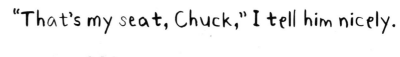
"That's my seat, Chuck," I tell him nicely.

"Oh, Katie," says Mom.
"You don't mind, do you?"

I do mind.
But I say it's okay,
and I move to Chuck's seat.

Sometimes I GRUMBLESQUINCH.

My insides **tighten** and I think mean thoughts.
I wish that I had a trampoline or a tree house or a giraffe
instead of a brother.
If I had one of those instead of a brother,
I could sit in my own seat at breakfast.

"Here's your bibble bibble," Dad says to Chuck.
Bibble bibble is what Chuck calls toast with butter.
Chuck doesn't like cereal.
Chuck only likes bibble bibble.

Chuck smashes his buttery fist into my bowl of cereal.

"Oh, Chuck! No punching Katie's cereal, silly,"
Mom says, putting him down on the floor.
"Say you're sorry to Katie."

I wish I could pop him like a balloon.
I wish he'd kaploom into a million bajillion
bibble bibble crumbs.
I wish he would disappear.

But I don't yell those wishes.
I GRUMBLESQUINCH them right down.

Chuck scampers over and grabs me with his milky hands.
He snuggles his buttery face against my beautiful new shirt.
I am a **tight**, horrible squinch of GRUMBLE.

"Chuck loves you!" Dad says.

He pulls Chuck off me and carries him away,
singing and smiling.

"You okay?" Mom asks me.
I nod because I am always okay.

But that nod is a lie.
I am not okay.

And lying about it is making me cry, and then

I just can't GRUMBLESQUINCH my feelings down anymore.

"Chuck ruins everything!"
I yell.
"He's sticky and stinky and
he breathes on me and
I want to sit in my own chair
and everybody smiles at him
but he is a buttery baby
on my shirt and
I wish I could Kaploom him UP!"

Then it's quiet.
I'm scared.
I didn't mean it.
But also, I did mean it.

They won't think I am such a pleasure anymore.

I wish I could GRUMBLESQUINCH it all back inside.
Maybe I ruined everything.

I wait for Mom to yell that I am bad.
To say, "YOU GO TO YOUR ROOM AND
THINK ABOUT IT!"
To look disappointed in me.

I look up at Mom's face.

"It's really hard sometimes,"
Mom whispers instead.
"Even when you love somebody."

I nod.
This nod is true.

Mom says, "I know."
She holds her arms out to me.

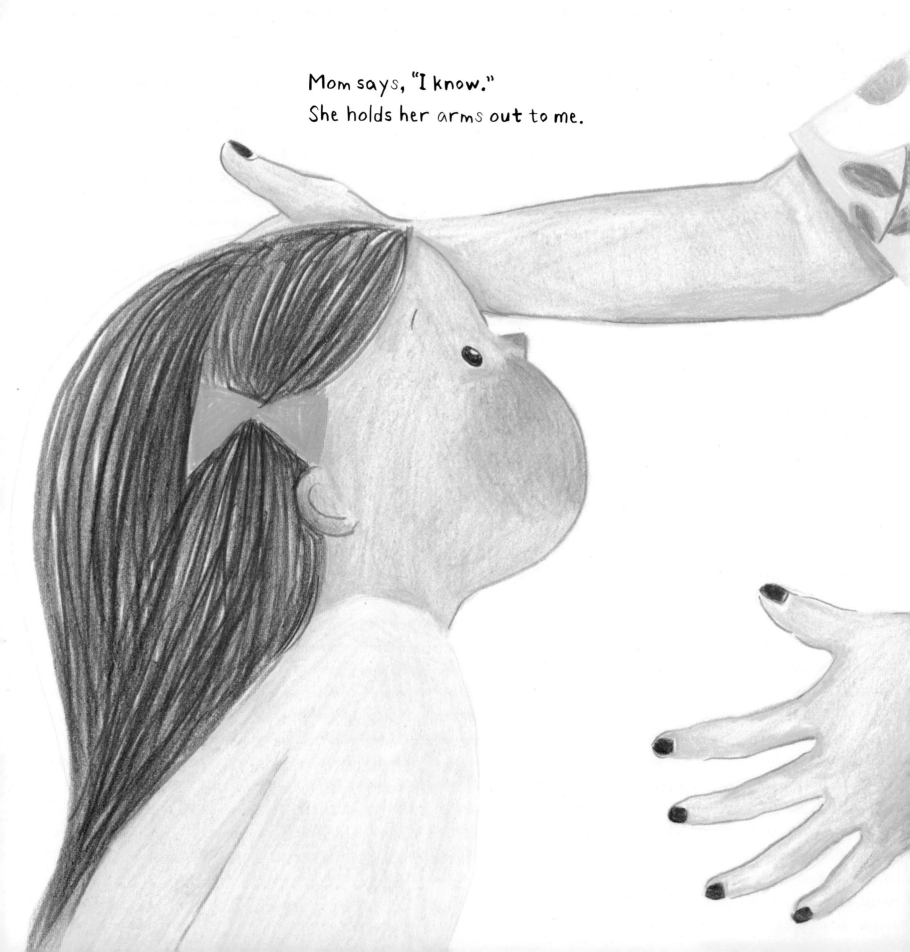

She folds me up safe in there.
I still fit perfectly.

Even though I didn't GRUMBLESQUINCH
all my secret thoughts inside.

There's room for the whole me.

Author's Note

When I was little (and even after I got bigger), it felt important to me to be a pleasure.
To be good.
To be well-behaved.
But also to be cheerful, happy, fine.

Most of the time that was pretty easy for me.
I actually felt that way!
But sometimes it was hard.
Sometimes I had grouchy feelings, or sad, frustrated, angry, even rageful or mean feelings.

How could a pleasant, easy, happy kid like me be feeling such things?
What would people think of me if I let those complex, confusing feelings out?

I didn't want to feel out of control.
And I certainly didn't want anyone to see me as nasty, cranky, bad.
So I taught myself to **Grumblesquinch** those negative emotions right down.

Do you ever **Grumblesquinch?**
It doesn't feel great, and it doesn't feel fully honest, right?
Also, it doesn't allow you to move past a troubling feeling.
Or even figure out why you're feeling that way.
Grumblesquinching is not a great solution, I decided.

But is the alternative to Kaploom?
To turn into Bombaloo whenever you have a big, challenging emotion?
I realized those are not the only choices.

Each of us has so many feelings.
Not all of them are pleasant.
We are all, every one of us, entitled to the full buffet of human emotions.

You are still you, and still lovable, even when you get frustrated or cranky, annoyed or sad.
You don't have to hold all that in, or hide it.
In fact, it's better if you can share what you're feeling with somebody.
Sharing honestly helps you cope.
There's room for the whole you, here.
I promise.

With love,
—Rachel Vail

Illustrator's Note

When I read the story, I immediately felt for Katie. As a child, I learned to tame my emotions. Often, I felt ashamed of having negative thoughts and I had to swallow my feelings. But in illustrating this book, I wanted to show that all those feelings are only natural. I used color pencils to highlight Katie's emotions. When she **Grumblesquinches**, her hair stands on end and the rainbow changes into a dark cloud. Her face turns red and pencil lines become quick and rough when she finally explodes. Still, in the end, the warm blanket of her mom's hugs tells us that it is okay to express how we really feel.

—Hyewon Yum

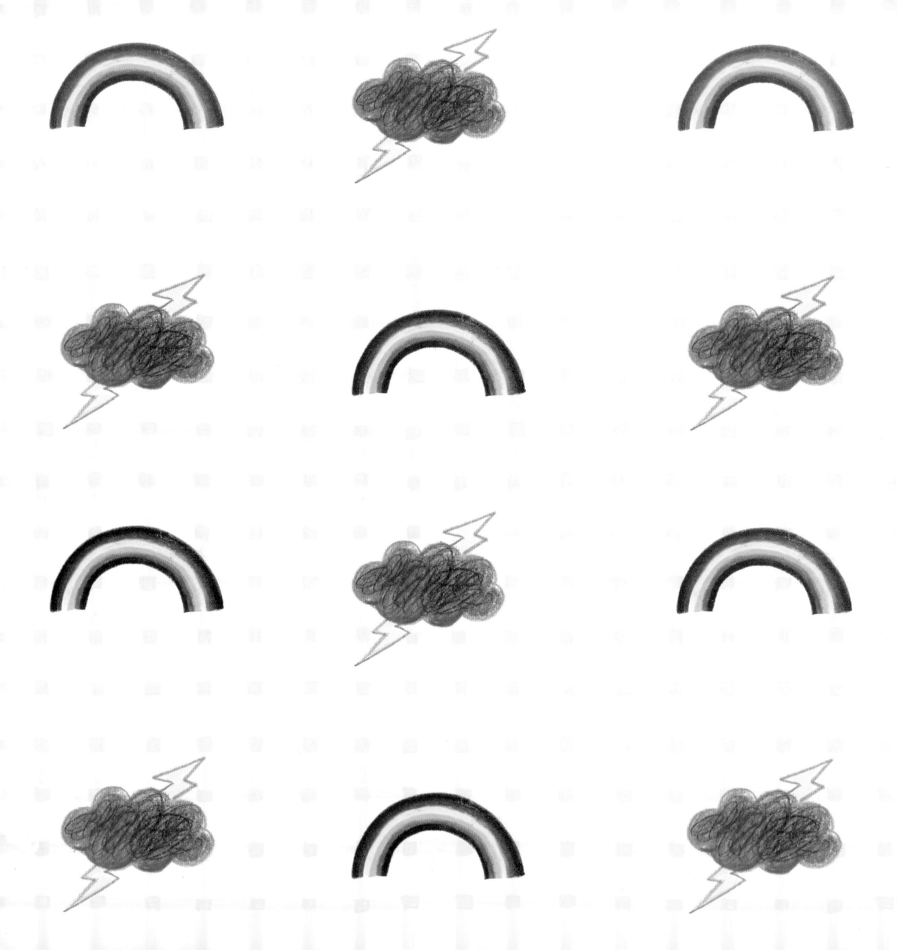